The boy who cried ninja

Alex Latimer

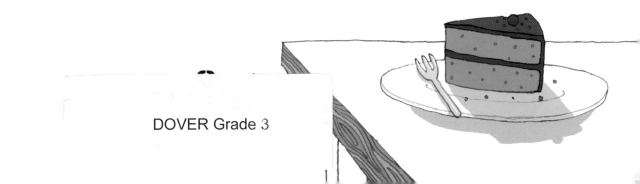

For Shann

Ω

Published by
PEACHTREE PUBLISHERS
1700 Chattahoochee Avenue
Atlanta, Georgia 30318-2112
www.peachtree-online.com

Originally published in Great Britain in 2011 by Random House.
First United States hardcover edition published in 2011
First United States trade paperback edition published in 2013

Artwork created as pencil drawings, digitized, then finished with color and texture

Printed in January 2017 in China
10 9 8 7 6 5 4 (hardcover)
10 9 8 7 6 (trade paperback)

Library of Congress Cataloging-in-Publication Data

Latimer, Alex.
The boy who cried ninja / written and illustrated by Alex Latimer.
p. cm.
Summary: A young boy named Tim is accused of lying when he tells his parents that a ninja ate the last piece of cake and a sunburned crocodile landed on the roof, so he figures out a way to prove that he is telling the truth.
ISBN 978-1-56145-579-9 (hardcover)
ISBN 978-1-56145-774-8 (trade paperback)
[1. Honesty—Fiction. 2. Humorous stories.] I. Title.
PZ7.L369612Bo 2011
[E]—dc22
2010034688

Once there was a boy named Tim
who no one believed.

When his mom asked him what happened to the last slice of cake, he told her the truth.

"It was a ninja," cried Tim.

First the ninja crept into the house

...then he kicked it into the air
and ate it in one bite.

When his dad asked him where the hammer was,
he told him the truth.

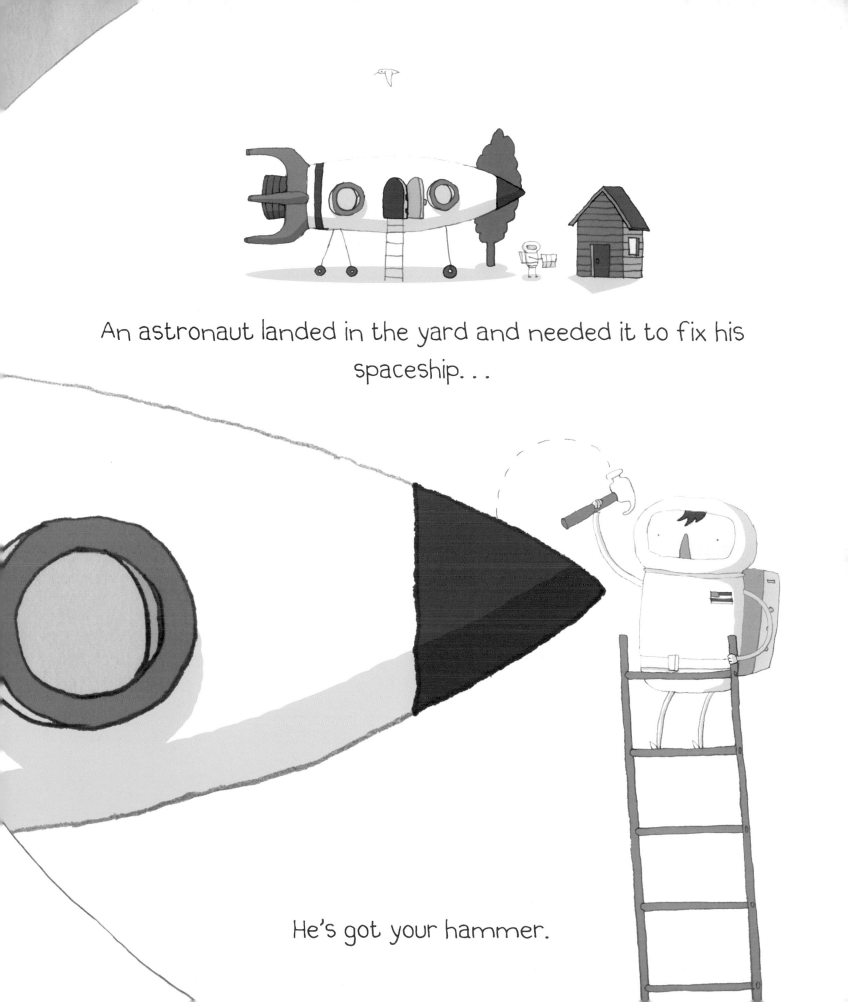

An astronaut landed in the yard and needed it to fix his spaceship. . .

He's got your hammer.

And when Grampa asked him if he'd done his homework,
Tim told him the truth.

A giant squid ate my whole book bag
while I was off buying an ice cream.

Tim's parents were very upset
with him for telling lies,

so they told him to go and rake up leaves
in the yard and think about what he'd done.

But the more he thought about it, the more he thought that maybe he really should lie.

Then no one would be mad at him.

So the next time a pirate jumped out of the cupboard . . .

and drank all the tea straight from the pot,

he owned up.

squawk

And the next time a sunburned crocodile
landed on the roof

and accidentally broke
the TV antenna

he confessed.

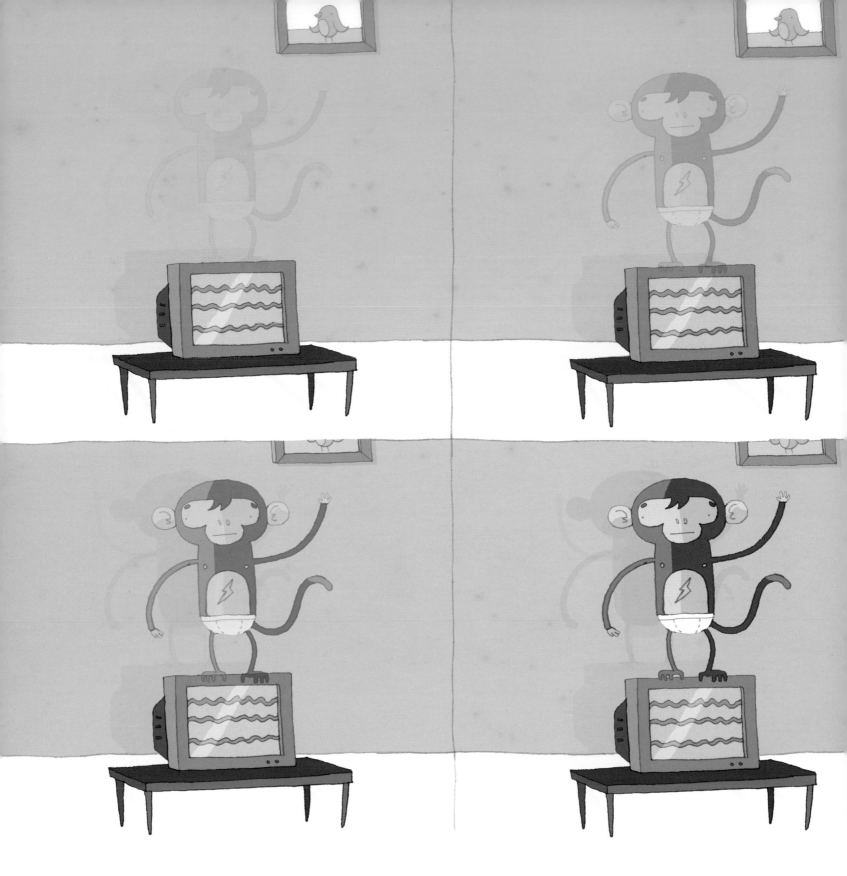

And the next time a time-traveling monkey
appeared on top of the TV

and started throwing pencils at Grampa
while he was sleeping,

OW!!

Tim said it was all his fault.

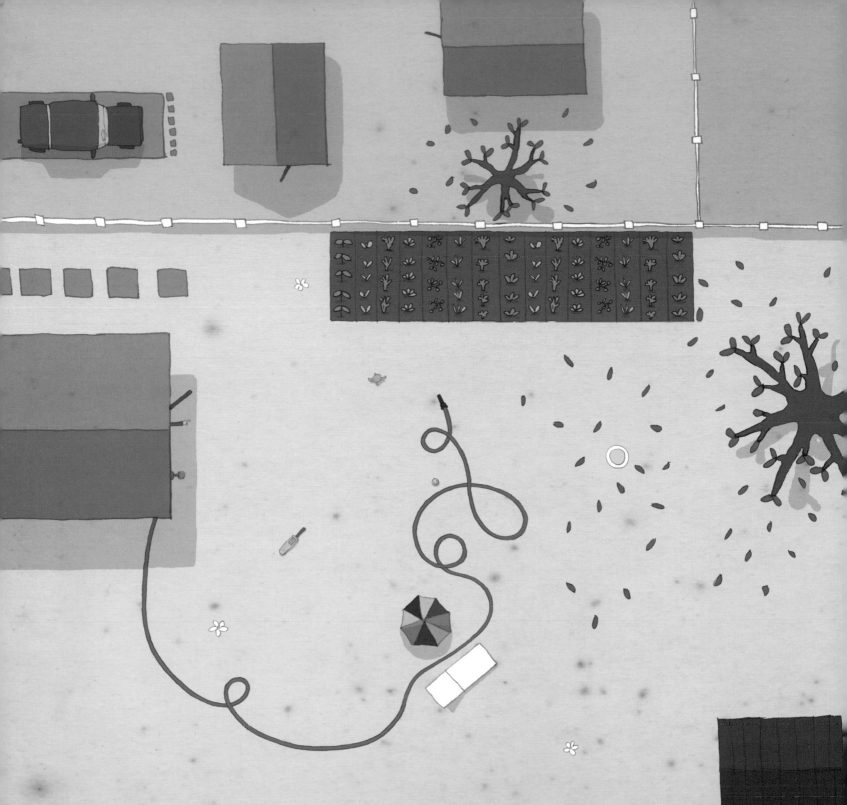

But none of that helped. Tim's parents told him
to go and water the vegetable garden
and think about all the bad things he'd done.

If he told the truth, he was in trouble,
and if he lied he was in trouble.
What could he do?

Then he had an idea.

He found some paper
and some stamps
and he wrote six letters:

Mr Squid
the ocean

Dear you,

there is a party at my house tomorrow. There will be plenty of cake, hammers, my new book bag, buckets of tea, TV antennas and pencils.

Please come.

Me

The next day was a Saturday. Dad was fixing the house,
Grampa was reading the newspaper, and Mom was vacuuming.

Then the doorbell rang. "Who could it be?" asked Grampa.
"I'll get it," said Tim.

There at the door stood a line of strange creatures.

First a ninja,

then an
astronaut,

a giant squid,

a pirate,

a crocodile
(recently recovered
from sunburn)

and a
time-traveling
monkey.

Tim's parents could see that he'd been trying
to tell the truth from the beginning. They said sorry
and promised to buy him a hundred ice creams.

As for the rest of them, Tim's parents were very upset.
"Go and rake all the leaves in the yard and think
about what you've done," said his dad.

When they had cleaned
the whole yard,
there really was a party.

And no one ate all the cake.
No one took anything without asking.
No one swallowed a book bag.
No one drank all the tea.
No one broke the antenna.
And no one threw pencils.

ta-da!

It was the best party Tim had ever had.

The End